One Girl

by
Andrea Beaty

illustrated by
Dow Phumiruk

Abrams Books for Young Readers
NEW YORK

One Girl.

One spark.

Faint and fading in the dark.

Flicker . . .

Flicker . . .

Flicker . . .

Glow.

Tiny ember.
Burning low.

One Girl.
One spark.

Glowing.
Growing in the dark.

Burning . . .

Burning....

Burning....

FIRE!

One Girl. Heart's desire.

Brighter.

Brighter.

Brightest bright.

One Girl

. . . in the light.

One Girl.
Growing strong.

One Girl glowing.

Shares her song.

Brighter.

Brighter.

Brightest bright.

Filled with wonder.

Heart takes flight.

Words like comets through the night.

Blazing streaks of blinding light.

Seeking out the darkest dark . . .

to bring one Girl

one shining
spark.

For my sister, Elizabeth
—A.B.
For my Mom and Dad, Suda and Soonthorn
—D.P.

Author's Note

Everything we have ever known or might ever imagine can be held between the covers of a book. That knowledge is a precious and powerful thing. Education shares that power and helps its recipients become their most amazing selves. But what if someone is kept from an education? That is the situation for over one hundred and thirty million girls around the world. Factors like poverty, political situations, remote living, violence, and child marriage keep girls out of classrooms and stop them from reaching their full potential. Global lack of education for girls hurts them, their families, their communities, and their countries. Educated girls grow into women who are healthier, earn higher incomes, and help the people in their lives out of poverty.

To learn more about how you can help girls around the world get an education, visit the United Nations Girls' Education Initiative (ungei.org) and donate to the Girls Opportunity Alliance (gofundme.com/c/girlsopportunityalliance).

The illustrations in this book were created with pencil and Photoshop.

Library of Congress Control Number 2019952287

ISBN 978-1-4197-1905-9

Text copyright © 2020 Andrea Beaty
Illustrations copyright © 2020 Dow Phumiruk
Book design by Pamela Notarantonio

Printed and bound in China
10 9 8 7 6 5 4 3 2

Abrams Books for Young Readers are available at special discounts when purchased in quantity for premiums
and promotions as well as fundraising or educational use. Special editions can also be created to specification.
For details, contact specialsales@abramsbooks.com or the address below.

Abrams® is a registered trademark of Harry N. Abrams, Inc.

ABRAMS The Art of Books
195 Broadway, New York, NY 10007
abramsbooks.com